W9-DFD-969

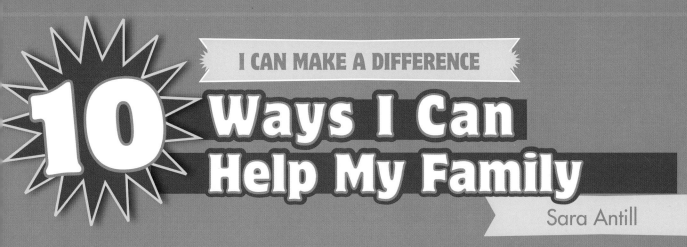

I CAN MAKE A DIFFERENCE

10 Ways I Can Help My Family

Sara Antill

PowerKiDS
press.
New York

Published in 2012 by The Rosen Publishing Group, Inc.
29 East 21st Street, New York, NY 10010

First Edition

Editor: Jennifer Way
Book Design: Ashley Drago

Photo Credits: Cover Sri Maiava Rusden/Getty Images; pp. 4–5 LWA/Dann Tardif/Getty Images; pp. 6–7 Ryan McVay/Digital Vision/Thinkstock; p. 8 David Sacks/Lifesize/Thinkstock; pp. 9, 18–19 Hemera/ Thinkstock; p. 10 Kraig Scarbinsky/Digital Vision/Thinkstock; p. 11 Lori Adamski Peek/Getty Images; pp. 12, 13, 14, 15, 20–21, 22 Shutterstock.com; pp. 16–17 © www.iStockphoto.com/Catherine Yeulet.

Library of Congress Cataloging-in-Publication Data

Antill, Sara.
  10 ways I can help my family / by Sara Antill. — 1st ed.
     p. cm. — (I can make a difference)
  Includes index.
  ISBN 978-1-4488-6204-7 (library binding) — ISBN 978-1-4488-6367-9 (pbk.) —
ISBN 978-1-4488-6368-6 (6-pack)
  1. Families—Juvenile literature. 2. Chores—Juvenile literature. 3. Housekeeping—Juvenile literature.
I. Title. II. Title: Ten ways I can help my family.
  HQ744.A825 2012
  173—dc23
                                        2011029811

Manufactured in the United States of America

CPSIA Compliance Information: Batch #WW12PK: For Further Information contact Rosen Publishing, New York, New York at 1-800-237-9932

Contents

Team Family!

What would happen if one member of a baseball team decided that he did not want to run the bases anymore? What if one member of a relay-race team decided not to run her part of the race? Team members must work together if they want to be successful. Families work like a team, too. Each member plays an important part in keeping a family safe and happy.

In this book, you will read about 10 things you can do to help your family. You can use these suggestions to improve the teamwork within your family.

Family teamwork makes household jobs easier and it makes family fun more enjoyable, too.

1 Keep Your Room Clean

When was the last time your parents told you to clean your room? Was it yesterday? Was it just a few minutes ago? Many kids feel like their parents are always asking them to clean their rooms.

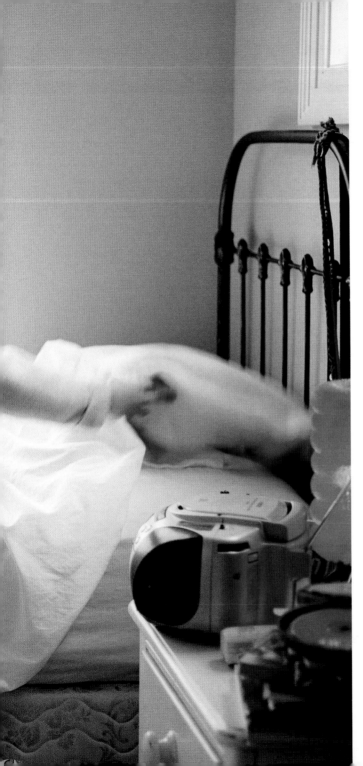

Leaving a few toys or books on your bedroom floor may not seem like a problem. However, it is easy for small messes to turn into big messes. Take a few minutes every day to tidy your room and you will never have to spend hours cleaning up. Best of all, the next time your parents see your room, they will probably say, "Good job!"

2 Help Around the House

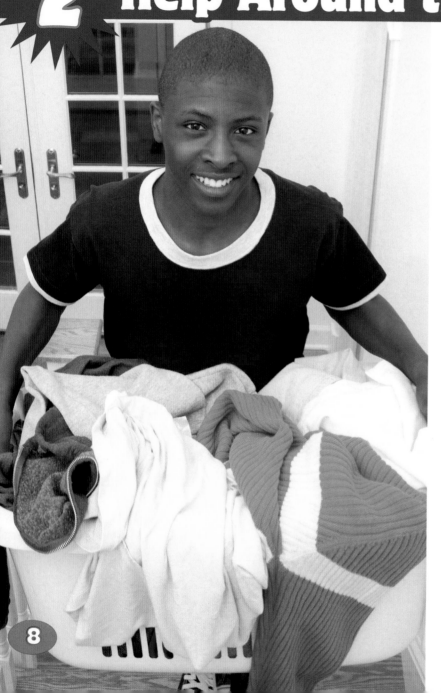

When a family is working together, each member has certain **chores**, or jobs to do around the house. Sit down with your parents and make a list of all the chores that need to be done. Then split the list between yourself, your parents, and your **siblings**.

> One of your chores might be to fold the clean laundry or to sort the dirty clothes for the wash.

If your family decides to do a chore wheel, you might clean the kitchen one week and the bathroom the next.

You can also make a chore wheel. Cut a large circle out of cardboard and put an arrow in the center that can spin. Draw lines to separate the circle into slices, like a pie, and write one chore in each slice. Each week, spin the arrow and trade chores!

3 Help with Dinner

Loading the dishwasher helps your family get the kitchen cleaned after dinner.

Between homework, jobs, and sports practices, it can be tough for a family to find a lot of time to spend together during the week. Dinner is a great chance for everyone in your family to come together. Making dinner for a family is a big job, though. You can help your family by helping with dinner!

Start by setting the table. Lay out a plate, fork, spoon, knife, and glass for each person. Ask an adult if you can help with the cooking by washing vegetables or peeling potatoes. After dinner, offer to clear the table or load the dishwasher.

Cleaning the vegetables and making a salad are ways you can help your family at dinnertime.

4 Help Your Siblings

You can also help your family by playing with your younger sibling.

Do you have any younger siblings? If so, you can help your family by helping your younger siblings! Try helping a younger sibling get ready for school. If you pour your own cereal for breakfast, pour some for your siblings at the same time.

5 Care for Your Pets

Having a pet is a big **responsibility**. Pets need food and water every day. You can learn about pet care by reading a book about animals or looking online. Dogs also need to be walked every day. Cats need to have their **litter boxes** cleaned. You can be a big help to your family by helping care for your pets.

Taking your dog for a walk is a good way to get some exercise. It is also a fun way to spend time with your pet.

6 Work in the Yard

Raking leaves in the fall can be a big job if your yard has a lot of trees. Family teamwork can make this job faster and more fun.

Lots of chores are done to take care of your house and keep it clean. Not all chores need to be done inside, though. There are outdoor chores, too. When the weather is warm, you can pull weeds or water plants. In the winter, you can shovel snow off the driveway. In the fall, you can rake leaves.

7 Wash the Car

Washing the car is a fun **activity** to do with your family. All you need is a bucket of water, sponges, and soap. One person can scrub the tires while another person washes the windows. By working together, you can quickly clean the car inside and out.

8 Start a Family Fun Night!

Do you like to play **board games** or card games? Many families set aside a night to spend time together and play games.

If not everyone in your family likes board games or card games, how about planning

an outdoor activity that everyone can enjoy. Is there a park nearby where you can go for a hike or ride bikes together? Maybe you can spend a night camping in the backyard. The most important thing is that your family spends time together and has fun. Family fun night is a good way for your family to **bond**.

Playing board games is a fun way to spend time with your family. It is also a good way to learn about teamwork and good sportsmanship.

9 Spend Time with Relatives

Do your grandparents live near you? Some kids have grandparents who live in the same house or town that they do. Others have grandparents who live far away.

If your grandparents or other older **relatives** live close by, plan some time to spend with them. You can go to the movies or just sit and talk. If your grandparents live far away, try to talk to them on the phone or online through **video chat**. Ask them to tell you about what life was like when they were kids. You may learn something exciting about your family that you did not know.

19

10 Have a Family Meeting

It is very important for family members to **communicate**, or share their thoughts, with each other. If one person has a problem, another member of the family may be able to help.

A great way to make sure everyone has a chance to share his or her feelings is to hold a **family meeting**. A family meeting lets everyone sit down together and take turns sharing. If there are any big changes coming for a family, such as a big move or a new baby, a family meeting is a good place for everyone to talk about their fears or excitement.

A family meeting is a time to share your feelings about what is going on. It is also a time to talk about your family's plans and goals.

Help the Team!

The best way to help your family is by being a good team member. In sports, good team members do not just play well. They help the other people on their team play well, too.

An important part of family teamwork is sharing household

Everyone in a family has his or her responsibilities. This helps the whole family work as a team.

responsibilities. Try to find ways to get your siblings excited about helping your parents around the house. Maybe you can join with other kids in your **neighborhood** and hold one big car wash, to which all of your parents can bring their cars. What other ways can you think of to help your family?

Glossary

activity (ak-TIH-vuh-tee) An action or a thing to do.

board games (BAWRD GAYMZ) Games that people can play together that are not played on computers or with cards.

bond (BOND) To form a close connection.

chores (CHORZ) Housework, or jobs that are done around the house.

communicate (kuh-MYOO-nih-kayt) To share facts or feelings.

family meeting (FAM-lee MEET-ing) A time when family members can talk about important things and share their feelings.

litter boxes (LIH-ter BOK-sez) The containers in which cats go to the bathroom.

neighborhood (NAY-ber-hud) A place where people live together.

relatives (REH-luh-tivz) People in the same family.

responsibility (rih-spon-sih-BIH-lih-tee) Something that a person must take care of or complete.

siblings (SIH-blingz) Sisters or brothers.

video chat (VIH-dee-oh CHAT) Talking with someone over the Internet using a video camera and a computer.

Index

Web Sites

Due to the changing nature of Internet links, PowerKids Press has developed an online list of Web sites related to the subject of this book. This site is updated regularly. Please use this link to access the list: www.powerkidslinks.com/diff/family/